W9-BAG-041

Gustave

Copyright © 2013 by Les Éditions de la Pastèque
Copyright © 2013 by Pierre Pratt (illustrations) & Rémy Simard (text)
First published in French in 2013 as *Gustave* by Les Éditions de la Pastèque, Montreal, Quebec
English translation copyright © 2014 by Groundwood Books
First published in English in Canada and the USA in 2014 by Groundwood Books

All rights reserved. No part of this publication may be reproduced, stored in a retrieval system or transmitted, in any form or by any means, without the prior written consent of the publisher or a license from The Canadian Copyright Licensing Agency (Access Copyright). For an Access Copyright license, visit www.accesscopyright.ca or call toll free to 1-800-893-5777.

Groundwood Books / House of Anansi Press
110 Spadina Avenue, Suite 801, Toronto, Ontario M5V 2K4
or c/o Publishers Group West
1700 Fourth Street, Berkeley, CA 94710

We acknowledge for their financial support of our publishing program the Canada Council for the Arts, the Government of Canada through the Canada Book Fund (CBF) and the Ontario Arts Council.

Canada Council   Conseil des Arts
for the Arts   du Canada

ONTARIO ARTS COUNCIL
CONSEIL DES ARTS DE L'ONTARIO

Library and Archives Canada Cataloguing in Publication
Simard, Rémy
[Gustave. English]
Gustave / written by Rémy Simard ; illustrated by Pierre Pratt ;
translation by Shelley Tanaka.
Translation of: Gustave.
Issued in print and electronic formats.
ISBN 978-1-55498-451-0 (bound). — ISBN 978-1-55498-452-7 (pdf)
I. Pratt, Pierre, illustrator II. Tanaka, Shelley, translator
III. Title. IV. Title : Gustave. English.
PS8587.I3065G8813 2014   jC843'.54   C2014-901345-0
C2014-902018-X

The illustrations were done in India ink and gouache and assembled digitally.
Printed and bound in Malaysia

MIX
Paper from
responsible sources
FSC® C012700
FSC
www.fsc.org

Gustave

Written by **Rémy Simard**   Pictures by **Pierre Pratt**

Translated by Shelley Tanaka

Groundwood Books / House of Anansi Press
Toronto Berkeley

He's gone.

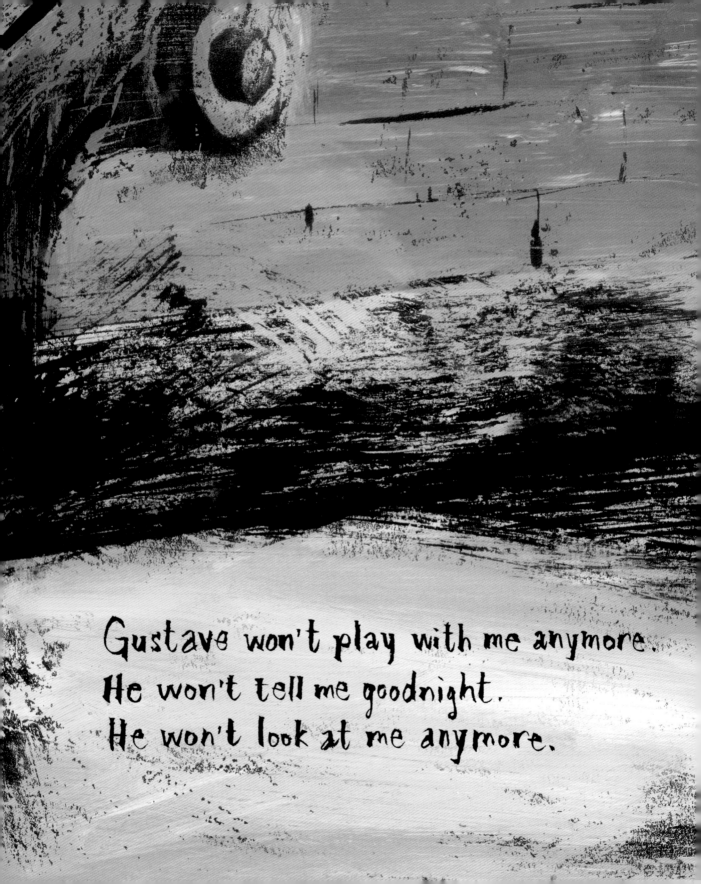

Gustave won't play with me anymore.
He won't tell me goodnight.
He won't look at me anymore.

The cat ate him.

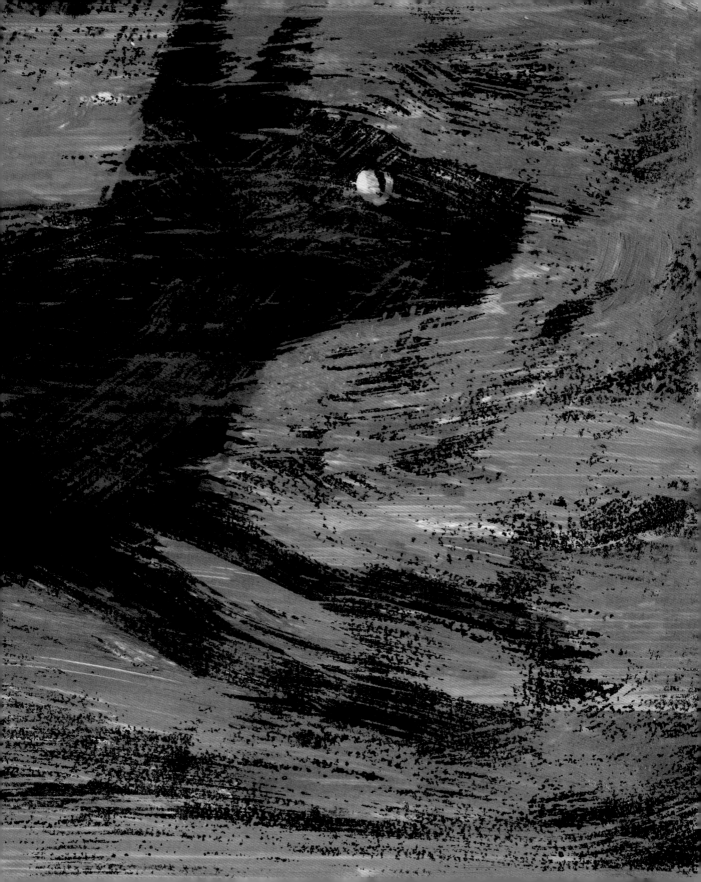

He surprised us.
We were playing when he
appeared right in front of us.

He was big and blue
with huge eyes.

He looked at Gustave,
and then he looked at me.

I screamed. I remember that.
And Gustave saved me.

I don't really know what happened.
He just made some little move.
Just enough for me to get away.

Run. Escape.

Disappear.

When I went back, the cat was gone.
And so was Gustave.

So I cried.
I cried all day long.
I couldn't go back home.
Not without Gustave.
What would I say to my mother?

She always told us not to go too far.
To play close to home.

But we didn't listen to her.
We always wanted to go farther.

And we did go farther and farther.
Mother warned us that there was
a cat.

It's late, I need to go home...

Mother is in the kitchen.
She's making dinner.
I look around me.
Gustave will never be here again.

Mother?

About Gustave...

Mother stops cooking.
She knows.

She hugs me tight.
"Poor Gustave. We loved him so much."
She lets me cry.

I cry some more. I cry a lot.
Then she takes me to her room.

She looks for something in her cupboard
and takes out a little stuffed mouse.
His eyes are shiny beads. His ears
are soft pink felt.
Just like Gustave's.
"His name is Harry," she says as
she hands him to me.

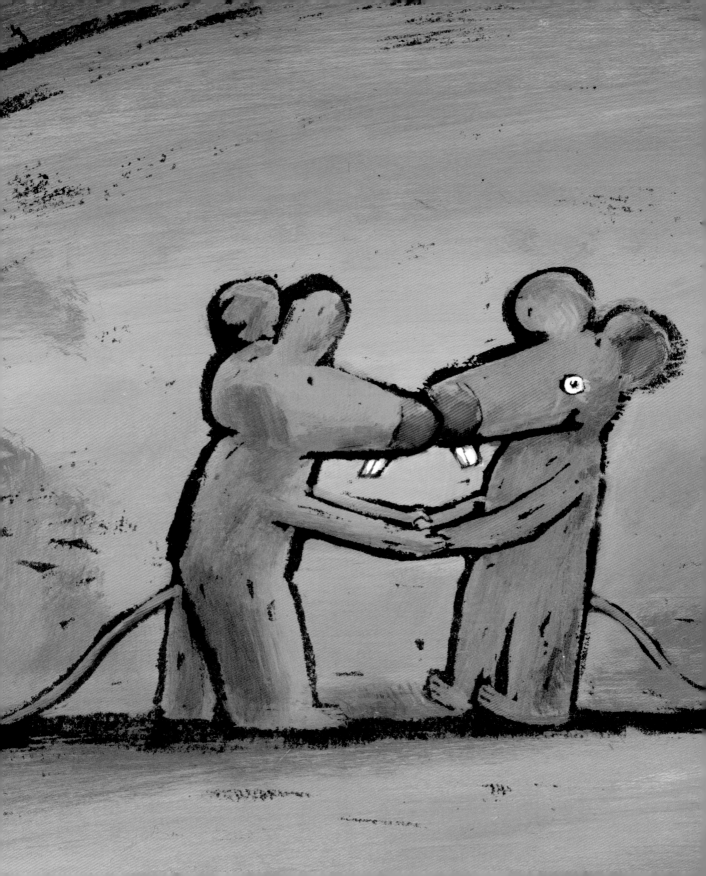

"You will never be Gustave,"
I tell him.

"I know," he seems to say.

We look at each other...

And I like him already.